U0060707

For Lesley

Speedy the TV Star

電視明星小快

Jill McDougall 著
王祖民 繪

Julie saw a sign in the window. It said:

Is your *pet smart?

Can your pet do *tricks?

Bring your pet to the TV station.

We will make your pet a TV star.

*為生字，請參照生字表

TV

Julie ran home to her pet turtle, Speedy.

"You are a smart turtle, Speedy," she said. "You will be a TV star."

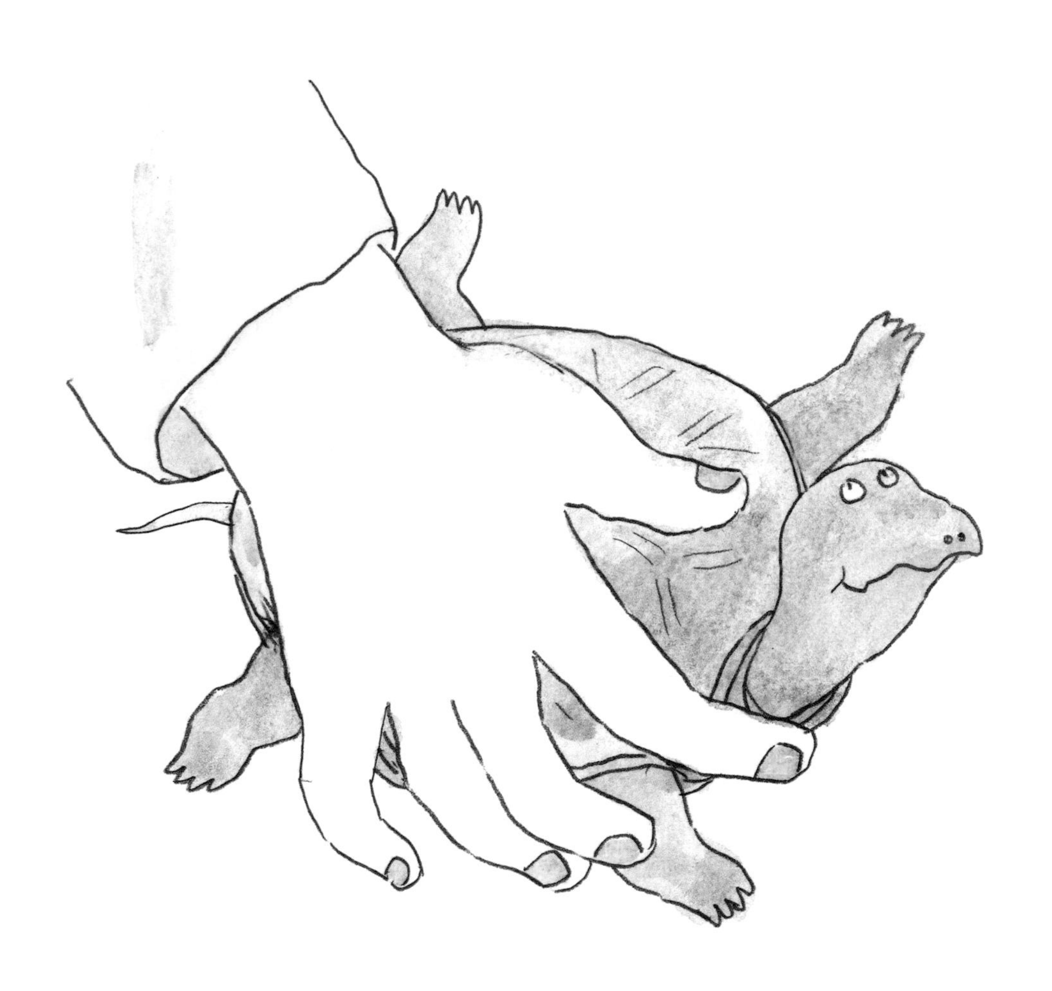

And off they went to the TV station.

The room was full of pets. There were big dogs and little dogs and black dogs and white dogs. There were big cats and little cats and black cats and white cats. There were rabbits and birds and mice.

But Speedy was the only turtle.

A little boy came over to look at Speedy in his *tank.

“What a cute turtle,” said the boy.

“This is Speedy,” said Julie. “And he is very smart.”

The TV man said, “All right, everyone. Let’s see what tricks your pet can do. The smartest pet will be on TV.”

The first pet was a big black dog.

He could shake hands.

“Good,” said the TV man.

The next pet was a
brown mouse.
She could run up
a *ladder.
"Very good," said
the TV man.

The next pet was a white cat.

She could dance on two legs.

"Great," said the TV man.

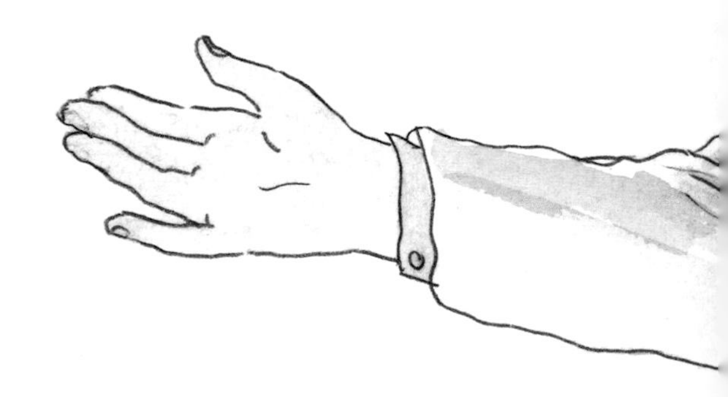

He looked at Julie.

“Now it is your turn,” he said.

Julie put Speedy on a rock. She *tapped the glass.

“Go on, Speedy,” said Julie. “Show the man your trick.”

Speedy swam to Julie.

"Is that all he can do?" said the TV man. "That's not a very good trick."

"He can do other things as well," said Julie.

"Show me later," said the TV man.

The next pet was a little brown dog.

She could jump very high.

"Good," said the TV man.

The next pet was a white rat.
She could *roll a ball along.
"Very good," said the TV man.

The next pet was a rabbit.
He could *hop in a circle.

"Great," said the TV man. He looked at Julie.

"You can have another *go now," he said.

Julie put Speedy on the table.

She gave him a *pea to eat.

"Go on, Speedy," said Julie.

"Show the man your trick."

Speedy looked all around the room.
Then he saw the pea and ate it.
“That’s not a very good trick,”
said the TV man. “You two can
go home.”
Julie felt very sad.
Speedy was not a TV star
after all.

Just then, the big black dog saw Speedy on the table.

He ran over.

*Clunk! Speedy rolled over. Then he went into his *shell and stayed very *still.

"Look at that!" said the TV man. "That turtle can *play dead."

Everyone *clapped.

"That's the best trick of all," said the TV man. "I will make this turtle a star."

"Good boy, Speedy," said Julie. "You will be on TV."

Speedy was still playing dead.

But Julie was sure he *winked at her!

生字表

p.2

pet [pεt] n. 寵物

trick [trɪk] n. 把戲；特技

p.8

tank [tæŋk] n.（用來盛裝液體的）箱，槽

p.11

ladder [`lædɚ] n. 梯子

p.14

tap [tæp] v. 輕拍，輕敲

p.17

roll [rol] v. 使滾動

hop [hɑp] v.（動物用）雙腳一起跳

p.18

go [go] n. 嘗試，機會

pea [pi] n. 豌豆

p.21

clunk [klʌŋk] v. 發出咚的一聲

shell [ʃεl] n. 殼

still [stɪl] adj. 靜止不動的

p.22

play dead 裝死

clap [klæp] v. 拍手，鼓掌

p.24

wink [wɪŋk] v. 眨眼

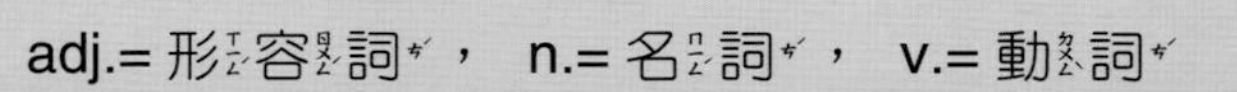

p.10

第ㄉㄧˋ一ㄧ隻ㄓ寵ㄔㄨㄥˇ物ㄨˋ是ㄕˋ隻ㄓ大ㄉㄚˋ黑ㄏㄟ狗ㄍㄡˇ，他ㄊㄚ會ㄏㄨㄟˋ握ㄨㄛˋ手ㄕㄡˇ。
電ㄉㄧㄢˋ視ㄕˋ台ㄊㄞˊ的˙ㄉㄜ人ㄖㄣˊ說ㄕㄨㄛ：「好ㄏㄠˇ。」

p.11

下ㄒㄧㄚˋ一ㄧ隻ㄓ寵ㄔㄨㄥˇ物ㄨˋ是ㄕˋ隻ㄓ棕ㄗㄨㄥ色ㄙㄜˋ的˙ㄉㄜ小ㄒㄧㄠˇ老ㄌㄠˇ鼠ㄕㄨˇ，她ㄊㄚ會ㄏㄨㄟˋ爬ㄆㄚˊ梯ㄊㄧ子ㄗˇ。
電ㄉㄧㄢˋ視ㄕˋ台ㄊㄞˊ的˙ㄉㄜ人ㄖㄣˊ說ㄕㄨㄛ：「非ㄈㄟ常ㄔㄤˊ好ㄏㄠˇ。」

p.12-13

接ㄐㄧㄝ下ㄒㄧㄚˋ來ㄌㄞˊ是ㄕˋ隻ㄓ白ㄅㄞˊ貓ㄇㄠ，她ㄊㄚ會ㄏㄨㄟˋ用ㄩㄥˋ兩ㄌㄧㄤˇ隻ㄓ腳ㄐㄧㄠˇ跳ㄊㄧㄠˋ舞ㄨˇ。
電ㄉㄧㄢˋ視ㄕˋ台ㄊㄞˊ的˙ㄉㄜ人ㄖㄣˊ說ㄕㄨㄛ：「太ㄊㄞˋ棒ㄅㄤˋ了˙ㄌㄜ。」
他ㄊㄚ看ㄎㄢˋ著˙ㄓㄜ茱ㄓㄨ莉ㄌㄧˋ說ㄕㄨㄛ：「現ㄒㄧㄢˋ在ㄗㄞˋ輪ㄌㄨㄣˊ到ㄉㄠˋ妳ㄋㄧˇ了˙ㄌㄜ。」

p.14

茱ㄓㄨ莉ㄌㄧˋ把ㄅㄚˇ小ㄒㄧㄠˇ快ㄎㄨㄞˋ放ㄈㄤˋ在ㄗㄞˋ石ㄕˊ頭ㄊㄡˊ上ㄕㄤˋ，然ㄖㄢˊ後ㄏㄡˋ拍ㄆㄞ拍ㄆㄞ玻ㄅㄛ璃ㄌㄧˊ。
茱ㄓㄨ莉ㄌㄧˋ說ㄕㄨㄛ：「來ㄌㄞˊ吧˙ㄅㄚ，小ㄒㄧㄠˇ快ㄎㄨㄞˋ。讓ㄖㄤˋ他ㄊㄚ看ㄎㄢˋ看ㄎㄢˋ你ㄋㄧˇ的˙ㄉㄜ本ㄅㄣˇ事ㄕˋ。」
小ㄒㄧㄠˇ快ㄎㄨㄞˋ游ㄧㄡˊ向ㄒㄧㄤˋ茱ㄓㄨ莉ㄌㄧˋ。

p.15

電視台的人說：「他就只會這樣嗎？那不算是個很棒的把戲喔。」
茱莉說：「他還會做別的事情。」
電視台的人說：「那等一下再表演給我看。」

p.16

下一隻寵物是隻棕色小狗，她能夠跳得很高。
電視台的人說：「好。」

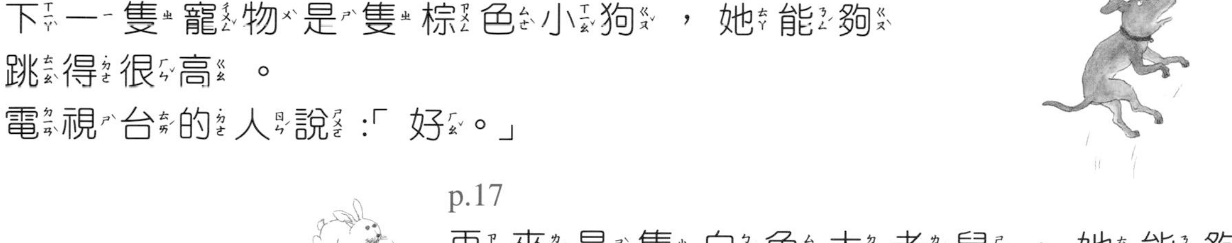

p.17

再來是隻白色大老鼠，她能夠一路滾著球跑。
電視台的人說：「非常好。」
接著是隻兔子，他會雙腳繞圈跳。

p.18

電視台的人說：「太棒了！」他看著茱莉說：「現在妳可以再來一次。」
茱莉把小快放在桌子上。
她給他吃一顆豌豆。
茱莉說：「來吧，小快。讓他看看你的本事。」

p.19

小快看看房間四周，然後他看到豌豆，就把它吃掉。

電視台的人說：「那不是個很好的把戲喔。你們兩個可以回家了。」

茱莉覺得很難過。小快終究不是個電視明星。

p.20-21

就在這時候，那隻大黑狗看見桌上的小快，就衝了過來。

「咚！」的一聲，小快整個身體翻了過來，然後縮進他的殼裡，一動也不動。

p.22

電視台的人說：「快看！那隻烏龜會裝死耶！」

大家都鼓掌了。

p.23

電視台的人說：「這是所有寵物把戲裡最棒的了。我要讓這隻烏龜變成電視明星。」

茱莉說：「小快，你真棒！你就要上電視了！」

p.24

小快還在裝死。

但是茱莉確定，小快對她眨了眨眼睛！

句型練習解答

② He can run very fast.
She cannot sing.
My brother can swim.
David cannot jump high.
I can play baseball.
We cannot dance.

句型練習

Someone Can....

在「電視明星小快」故事中，我們看到了許多有關“Speedy can....”（小快能……）的用法，現在我們就來練習“Someone can....”（某人可以……）的句型吧！

① 請跟著 CD 的 Track 4，唸出下面這些表示「動作」的英文

play baseball

dance

run very fast

sing

swim

jump high

② 請仔細聽 CD 的 Track 5 ，利用左頁的提示完成以下的句子：

Speedy can swim.

Speedy can eat a pea.

Speedy cannot hop in a circle.

Speedy cannot jump.

He can ____________.

She cannot ____________.

My brother can ____________.

David cannot ____________.

I can ____________.

We cannot ____________.

龜殼的三大秘密

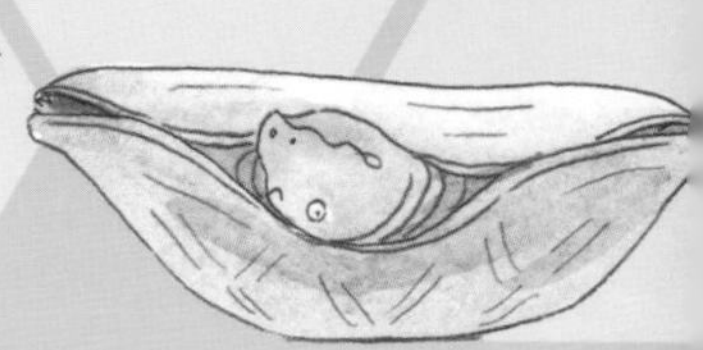

烏龜的龜殼是身體最重要部份，除了有美麗的花紋之外，還透露了一些烏龜的祕密喔！

1. 保護功能

遇到危險時，烏龜保護自己的方式，就是像小快一樣，把頭、四肢跟尾巴縮到自己的龜殼裡，這樣一來，想要攻擊牠的敵人既沒有辦法抓牠出來，又奈何不了牠硬梆梆的殼，也只能望殼興嘆，最後拍拍屁股走掉了。

不過，烏龜縮頭的方法會隨著種類而有所不同喔！比較常見的是把頭直接往後縮到龜殼裡的「隱頸龜」；另一種叫「側頸龜」，因為牠沒辦法直接把脖子往殼裡縮，所以只能儘量彎著脖子，讓脖子緊緊貼在肩膀的一側，好把頭藏在龜殼的邊緣。

2. 年齡和性別

　　龜殼其實隱藏了很多訊息。比如說，我們要怎麼知道烏龜幾歲了呢？只要觀察烏龜的「背甲」——也就是牠背上的殼，就可以看到一圈一圈的紋路，紋路越多，就表示牠的年紀越大。還有，也可以藉著觀察牠們的「腹甲」——也就是烏龜的肚子，來分辨這隻烏龜是公的還是母的喔！一般來說，雌烏龜的腹甲是平坦的，而雄烏龜的則會往內凹。

3. 健康狀況

　　雖然龜殼看起來好像很堅硬，可是如果你對它太粗魯，它還是可能會裂開，所以千萬不要試著拿東西去敲它。另外，如果你發現烏龜的殼變得軟軟的，就表示牠生病了，這時要多餵牠吃含豐富鈣質的食物，並且讓牠多曬曬太陽，也別忘了帶牠去看醫生喔！

Fun心讀雙語叢書

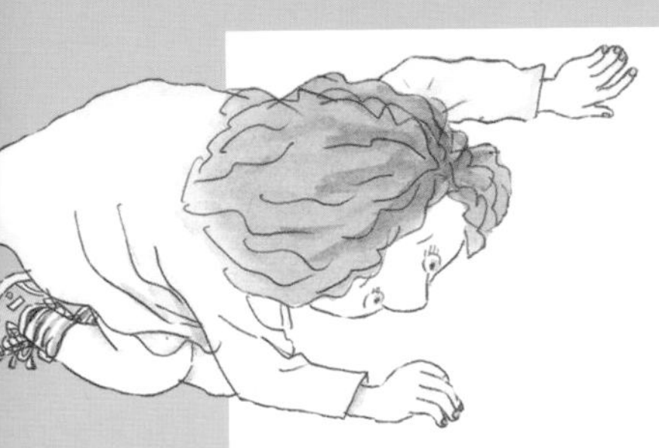

小烏龜大麻煩系列
Turtle Trouble Series

Jill McDougall 著／王祖民 繪

附中英雙語朗讀CD／適合具基礎英文閱讀能力者(國小4-6年級)閱讀

① 貪吃的烏龜小快 (Speedy the Greedy Turtle)
② 小快的比賽 (Speedy's Race)
③ 小快上學去 (Speedy Goes to School)
④ 電視明星小快 (Speedy the TV Star)
⑤ 怎麼啦，小快？ (What's Wrong, Speedy?)
⑥ 小快在哪裡？ (Where Is Speedy?)

烏龜小快是小女孩茱莉養的寵物，他既懶散又貪吃，還因此鬧出不少笑話，讓茱莉一家人的生活充滿歡笑跟驚奇！想知道烏龜小快發生了什麼事嗎？快看《小烏龜大麻煩系列》故事，保證讓你笑聲不斷喔！

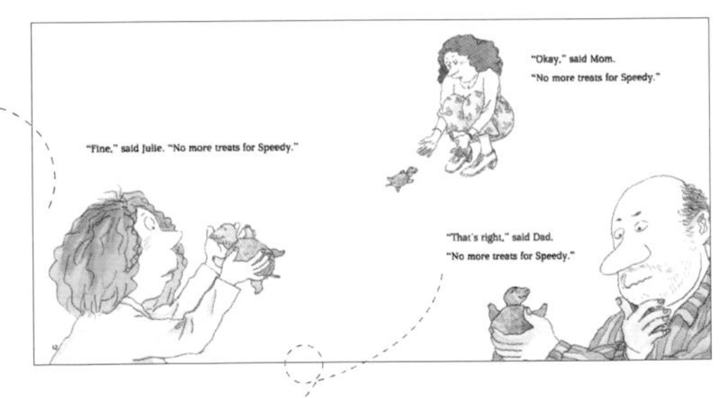

活潑可愛的插畫
還有突破傳統的編排方式
視覺效果令人耳目一新

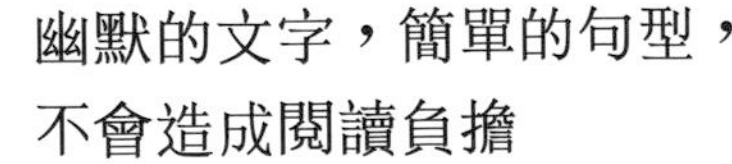

幽默的文字，簡單的句型，
不會造成閱讀負擔

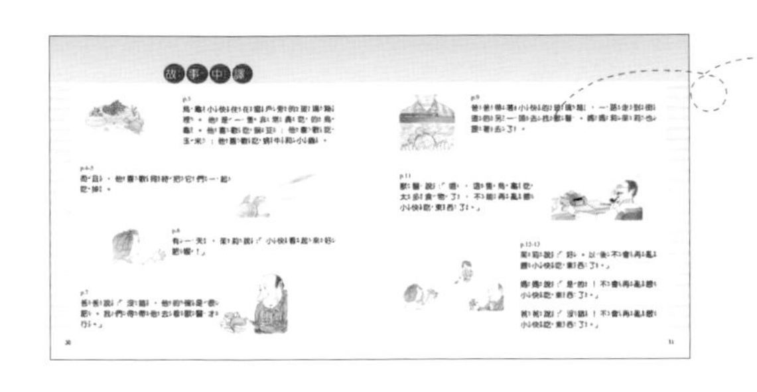

故事中譯保持英文原味，又可當成完整的中文故事閱讀

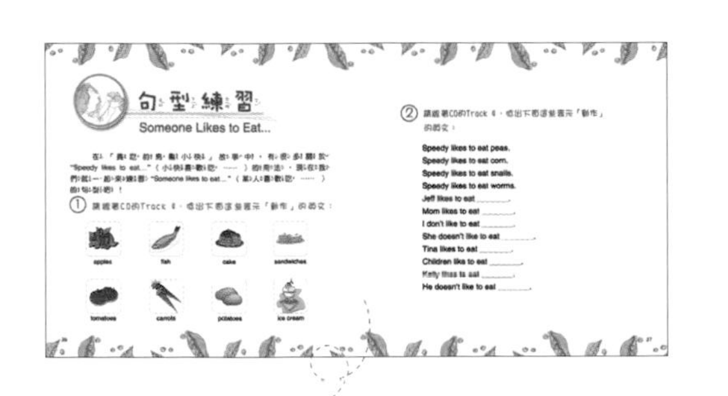

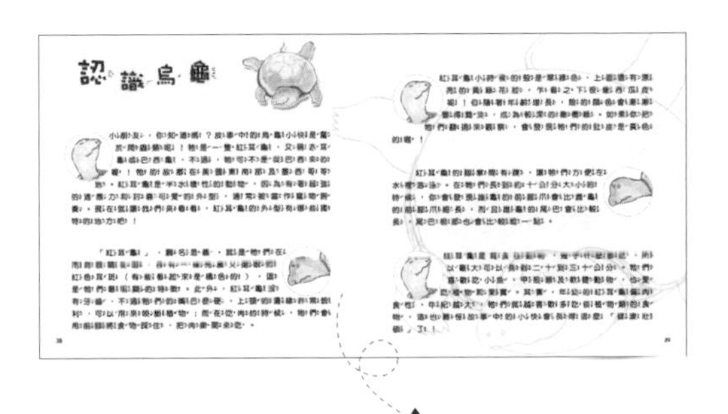

書後附英文句型練習，加強讀者應用句型能力，幫助讀者融會貫通

補充與故事有關的小常識，讓讀者更了解故事內容

附英文生字表，幫助讀者了解故事內容

Fun心讀雙語叢書
小老鼠貝貝歷險記系列
Tabitha and the Elephants
Marc Ponomareff　著／王平，倪靖，郜欣　繪／本局編輯部　譯
精裝／附中英雙語朗讀CD／全套六本
一隻機智勇敢的小老鼠，一隻真誠可愛的象寶寶，
六本為孩子量身打造的雙語繪本，
讓你在一連串驚險刺激的冒險故事中學英文！
① Tabitha Meets An Elephant　貝貝與小潔的相遇
② Tabitha and the Laughing Hyenas　小老鼠貝貝與土狼
③ Tabitha and the Python　小老鼠貝貝與大蟒蛇
④ Tabitha and the Crocodile　小老鼠貝貝與鱷魚
⑤ Tabitha Escapes from the Lions　小老鼠貝貝逃生記
⑥ A Party for Tabitha　小老鼠貝貝的驚喜派對

國家圖書館出版品預行編目資料

Speedy the TV Star:電視明星小快 / Jill McDougall 著;王祖民繪;本局編輯部譯.－－初版一刷.－－臺北市：三民，2005
面；　公分.－－(Fun心讀雙語叢書.小烏龜，大麻煩系列④)
中英對照
ISBN 957-14-4326-3　(精裝)
1. 英國語言－讀本
523.38　　94012417

網路書店位址　http://www.sanmin.com.tw

© Speedy the TV Star
——電視明星小快

著作人　Jill McDougall
繪　者　王祖民
譯　者　本局編輯部
發行人　劉振強
著作財產權人　三民書局股份有限公司
臺北市復興北路386號
發行所　三民書局股份有限公司
地址／臺北市復興北路386號
電話／(02)25006600
郵撥／0009998-5
印刷所　三民書局股份有限公司
門市部　復北店／臺北市復興北路386號
重南店／臺北市重慶南路一段61號
初版一刷　2005年8月
編　號　S 805611
定　價　新臺幣壹佰捌拾元整
行政院新聞局登記證局版臺業字第〇二〇〇號

有著作權・不准侵害

ISBN 957-14-4326-3　(精裝)